MW01671050

First Lights of Mahone Bay: A Harborlights Seasons Prequel

Sylvia Price

Published by Penn and Ink Writing, LLC, 2026.

This is a work of fiction. Similarities to real people, places, or events are entirely coincidental.

FIRST LIGHTS OF MAHONE BAY: A HARBORLIGHTS SEASONS PREQUEL

First edition. February 24, 2026.

ISBN: 979-8233845338

Written by Sylvia Price.

Table of Contents

Chapter One

The road leading into Mahone Bay narrowed as Marissa Clarke drove, the pavement curving gently as if sensing her reluctance to accept her circumstances, guiding her and gradually ushering her toward her destination. The colorful houses that dotted the roadside were painted in soft pastels, and weathered hues gave the impression more of a painting than an actual scene. The pale blue reminded her of sea glass, the butter yellow of gentle warming sunlight. The faded rose, softened by salt air and years of storms, brought Turkish Delight to mind. They stood on the street edges, companionably sharing secrets she wasn't yet invited to hear as an outsider.

She slowed involuntarily, her tightening hands on the steering wheel turning ashen. The air smelled different in Mahone Bay—salt and pine, with a hint of sweetness that was familiar yet unplaceable. It wasn't sharp like the ocean air she associated with crowded boardwalks and tourist beaches. It was softer. Quieter. Like a breath released gently rather than expelled with force.

This is it, she thought.

Day one. Just arrival. Just breathing. Nothing had to be decided yet. Her stomach fluttered and flipped with equal excitement and fear. The body's innate response to being at the edge of a moment that could change everything.

She glanced in the rearview mirror as she idled at a stop sign near the waterfront and saw her own eyes staring back at her. They looked tired—too jaded for someone her age. She'd grown used to the fatigue, worn it like a heavy garment she never removed. In the city, with the fast pace of life, it had been normal to feel constantly behind, constantly late, constantly proving something. Now, the tiredness felt like a stranger in the passenger seat.

As she turned onto the road that hugged the harbor, she passed a small marina where sailboats bobbed lazily in the water. Their halyards clinked against the masts in a faint melodic rhythm—soft metal against metal, like the ocean's wind chimes. Folks moved along the docks, unhurried, greeting one another with waves and nods that bespoke familiarity. Everyone appeared to be confident in their belonging.

Her tires crunched over the gravel as she pulled into a small parking lot near the waterfront. She just sat there momentarily, engine idling, pulse pounding loudly in her ears. Her car was filled with the remnants of her former life: a city apartment reduced to boxes and bags, stacked neatly. Evidence of a choice she had made in a moment of quiet desperation and stubborn hope.

Marissa let her gaze drift to the passenger seat, where her planner lay, closed but heavy with meaning. A muted gray cover. No personality. No softness. Just efficiency. She picked it up, turning it in her hands like an artifact from a life she wasn't sure she still recognized.

For three years, her planner was her anchor. Color-coded deadlines and endless meetings. She had been good at it. Too good. In the city, competence had been her currency. She delivered on time. She smoothed conflicts before they became problems. She filled in gaps no one else noticed because it was easier than being the one who caused friction.

Excellence had made her reliable. And reliability, in turn, made her invisible.

She remembered the conference room clearly. The long white table. The smell of burnt coffee. The way her proposal had been projected on the screen—her words, research, hours of work distilled into bullet points.

She had explained it calmly. Confidently. And then, minutes later, someone else repeated her idea in a louder voice with sharper certainty.

Followed by the moment the entire room leaned forward, and her manager said,

"That's exactly what we need."

Not to her. To him.

Marissa had sat there, hands folded, pulse steady on the outside while something hollowed inside her.

Later, in the elevator, she had caught her reflection in the mirrored wall and realized no one in the building could describe her beyond what she produced.

She was useful. She was capable. She was replaceable.

Her phone buzzed again. The message icon waited.

Please confirm you've handed off the client files.

No greeting. No hesitation. Just expectation.

She turned the phone face down.

She hadn't left the city because it was cruel. She left because it was indifferent. Because no one there would notice if she stopped showing up, as long as the work continued.

Marissa placed the planner back on the seat, but it was no longer her lifeline. Rather, it was a record of who she once was, not a contract for who she had to remain.

Outside her car, Mahone Bay waited.

Salt and pine instead of toner and glass.

She pressed her palm to the steering wheel, steadying herself.

"I'm not running," she whispered. "I'm choosing."

And for the first time in a long while, the words felt true.

She turned off the engine and stepped out. The breeze caught her hair instantly, lifting and fingering the golden strands, brushing them against her cheeks. She closed her eyes and inhaled deeply. The scents of salt and woodsmoke and fresh bread wrapped around her in an unexpected welcome.

The harbor stretched before her, sunlight skittering across the water in a thousand trembling reflections. The early morning sky was a pale blue brushed with streaks of soft gold. The town was slowly waking, with no sense of urgency. Without pressure. A place where time had learned to be patient.

She grabbed her jacket from the passenger seat and slipped it on even though the air was warmer than she'd expected. Habit, she supposed. Armor, maybe. Something to keep her grounded when everything else felt so uncertain.

Her phone buzzed again. A message from her sister.

Did you make it?

Marissa smiled faintly as she typed back.

Just arrived. It's...beautiful.

She hesitated before adding,

And terrifying.

She slipped the phone into her pocket and started walking toward the row of shops lining the waterfront. Hand-painted signs hung above doors: a bookstore, a café, a florist, a small artisan market. Everything looked curated but not artificial. Lived-in. Loved. There were flower boxes even in winter—hardy greens tucked around small bursts of color—like the town saw every season as a time for celebration.

Marissa paused in front of the café.

"Harborlight Café & Bakery," the sign read, painted in warm curvy white letters against a navy background. Through the large front window, in the soft yellow light, she could see a chalkboard menu written in looped handwriting. A woman behind the counter laughed at something someone had said, her voice carrying faintly through the glass.

Marissa's chest tightened with longing.

Connection. Belonging. The things she'd convinced herself she didn't need but never truly stopped wanting.

Not yet, she thought. *One step at a time.*

She turned from the café and continued down toward the marina, wanting to explore before her nerves convinced her to retreat into her car and drive away. The docks were quiet but not empty. A man in a knit cap coiled rope with practiced calm. Another scrubbed the deck of a small fishing boat, humming softly.

No one looked rushed. No one looked lost.

She wondered how long it took to become that settled.

Her foot caught on a loose board as she stepped onto the dock. She wobbled, catching herself just in time, her heart jumping into her throat.

"Smooth," she muttered.

A laugh bubbled nearby. Low, warm, not unkind.

She looked up, startled.

A man stood a few yards away, holding a crate of supplies against his hip. He was tall, broad-shouldered without being imposing, dressed in worn jeans and a faded gray hoodie. Dark hair curled beneath a navy knit cap, and his eyes—she registered distantly that they were a striking shade of hazel—crinkled at the corners as he smiled.

"First day on the docks?" he asked, his eyes twinkling in amusement.

"That obvious?" she volleyed back, her sarcasm effectively masking her embarrassment.

"The wobble gave it away. But hey, you didn't fall in. That's better than most."

She smiled despite herself. "I'll aim higher next time."

He shifted the crate to his other arm. "Welcome to Mahone Bay."

Something about the way he said it—like a statement rather than a question—made her chest tighten. "Thank you. I just arrived."

"New in town, then."

"Yes." She tucked a strand of hair behind her ear. "Is it always this...peaceful?"

He paused to consider his answer. "Most days. Storms come and go, but we don't forsake the calm just because they exist."

She liked that. She liked it far more than she wanted to admit.

"Well," she said. "I hope I learn how to do that."

He smiled again, slower. "You will."

"I'm Marissa," she said.

He hesitated for just a beat. "Caleb."

She repeated his name softly, and he felt something warm shift in his chest—dangerous, familiar.

There was a pause. Not awkward, exactly. Just...unfinished.

"I should—" She gestured vaguely toward the street. "I have a rental to check into."

"Right," he said. "If you need anything, ask around. Someone will point you in the right direction."

"Thank you," she replied with a grateful smile.

He nodded once, already turning back toward his task. "Enjoy your first day."

She walked away with her pulse still uneven, her thoughts strangely scattered. The encounter had been brief, insignificant on the surface. And yet, it lingered—like the echo of a song she hadn't realized she wanted to hear.

• • • •

THE RENTAL, SMALL, white, and tucked behind a row of spruce trees, was close enough to the water that she could hear the sounds of the sea and harbor if she stood still long enough. Inside, it smelled faintly of lemon cleaner and old wood. Simple furniture. Soft blue curtains. A narrow bed and a tiny kitchen that looked as though it had been built for someone who didn't intend to stay long.

She set her bags down and stood in the middle of the room, suddenly aware of the quiet.

Not the peaceful quietude of the harbor but the personal quietness of being entirely unknown.

No one there knew her habits. No one expected her. No one would notice if she stayed in all evening or left town before morning.

She unpacked slowly, placing clothes into drawers, lining her toiletries on the bathroom counter, arranging her sketchbook and journal on the small desk by the window. Each small act felt like a question.

Am I really doing this?

She found herself standing in front of the narrow closet, holding a framed photo she'd wrapped in a sweater. Her sister, laughing at some joke Marissa had already forgotten. Taken two years earlier at a work event Marissa had almost skipped. She set it on the small nightstand, the only personal item in the room that belonged to her and not the generic space.

In the kitchen, she perused the cupboards, finding mismatched mugs and plates that had probably served dozens of short-term renters. She filled the kettle—an old-fashioned one that sat on the stove—and listened to the tick of the burner as it heated. While waiting, she sliced an apple from the grocery bag she'd picked up on the way into town. The knife was dull, the cutting board scarred with years of use.

Everything in the cottage had a history she wasn't part of yet.

The kettle whistled. She made tea and carried it to the window, watching the light change as afternoon shifted toward evening. The harbor turned gold, then amber, then a deep blue that made the water look almost black. Lights appeared in windows across the bay—small yellow squares that felt both distant and intimate.

Marissa's thoughts turned to her apartment in the city. The view had been of another adjacent building, close enough that she could see into other people's lives without ever being a part of them. She'd kept her blinds closed most of the time. The rental's windows had thin white curtains that barely filtered the light, as if privacy was less of a priority than connection.

Her phone buzzed. An email. This one from a coworker—someone she'd worked beside for three years whose last name she had to think about before remembering.

Hope you're settling in! We miss you already!

The superficiality of it stung less than it once would have. She set the phone face-down again and took a sip of tea.

Outside, a couple walked past on the street below, their voices carrying in the quiet evening air. She couldn't make out the words, only the rhythm of easy conversation. One of them laughed—a warm, unguarded sound.

In the city, she'd learned to make herself small. Efficient. Unobtrusive. The kind of person who didn't take up space or require accommodation.

In Mahone Bay, she wasn't sure what was expected. And somehow, that felt like freedom.

She finished her tea standing at the window, watching Mahone Bay settle into night. The doubt was still there—sharp and familiar. But beneath it, something else was beginning to take root.

Not confidence. Not certainty.

Just the smallest whisper of maybe.

The doubt returned as darkness fell. She could leave. She could call this a scouting trip, tell herself she was gathering impressions, not making decisions. She could drive back to a life that already knew her name—even if it only used it when it needed something.

Marissa pressed her palms to her knees and stared out the window at the distant gleam of water.

She remembered the voice of the man, Caleb, at the marina.

We don't forsake the calm just because storms exist.

It wasn't romantic. It was something steadier than that: the idea that calm could be protected. Chosen. Learned.

She wasn't ready to belong yet.

But for the first time in a long while, she was ready to stay long enough to try.

• • • •

CALEB MOORE WATCHED her go. Not in an intrusive way. Just long enough to make sure she didn't trip again. Or get lost. Or look back.

She didn't.

Newcomers always stood out like sore thumbs. They exuded a certain tension, a cautious hope that reminded him of unopened letters. He usually kept his distance. It was easier not to invest in people who might not stay.

But something about her—about the way she had taken in the harbor like it was a promise rather than a postcard—made him pause.

Mahone Bay had a way of deciding who belonged.

And for reasons he couldn't yet explain, he had a feeling she might be one of them.

Chapter Two

The next couple of days passed in a blur of unpacking and nervous exploration. Marissa walked the streets twice, memorizing shop names and the rhythm of the tides. She ate takeout alone in her rental and reassured herself she was adjusting, not hiding.

By the third morning in Mahone Bay, the screech of permanently hungry gulls and the distant lapping of water against wood had become almost familiar to the point of habituation, where they no longer registered each time she heard them. The morning's light filtered through thin white curtains, casting soft shadows across the simple furniture.

She sat up slowly, listening. No sirens. No traffic rushing past. Only the quiet rhythm of a town beginning another ordinary day.

She padded over to the window. The harbor shimmered in early light, serene and steady. Boats rocked gently. A man walked along the docks carrying something heavy with practiced ease. The town was already moving, but it wasn't hurrying.

That helped.

She carefully chose a soft sweater and jeans as her outfit, wanting to look like she belonged even if she didn't quite feel it yet. As she brushed her hair, she caught her reflection in the mirror and paused. There was something different in her eyes. Not confidence. Not certainty. But openness—as if she had finally allowed herself to want something without instinctively immediately planning how to protect herself from it.

The Harborlight Café felt warmer than it had looked through the window two days prior. The bell above the door chimed softly as she stepped inside, and the scent of cinnamon, coffee, and fresh pastry welcomed her like long-lost friends.

A young woman with dark curls looked up and smiled. "Good morning! First time here?"

Marissa chuckled. "Do I stick out?"

"Only in the best way. I'm Sophie."

"Marissa."

"Well, welcome to Mahone Bay, Marissa. What can I get you?"

She ordered a coffee and a blueberry scone and chose a seat by the window, observing the marina while the café filled with soft conversation around her. People greeted one another by name. Someone called out a reminder about a church fundraiser. Another person mentioned needing help fixing a porch railing.

No one sounded rushed. No one sounded lonely.

She wrapped her hands around her mug and let the warmth seep into her. For the first time since arriving, she wasn't bracing herself for something. She was simply present.

She finished her coffee slowly, savoring it while watching the light change on the water. When she finally stood to leave, Sophie called out, "See you tomorrow?"

The assumption startled her—and pleased her.

"Maybe," Marissa answered, smiling.

"I'll take that as a yes."

Outside, the morning had reached full brightness. She sauntered toward the marina without conscious decision, her feet following the path she'd taken on her first day.

She paused near the docks to study a laminated map mounted on a wooden post; a familiar voice spoke behind her.

"Lost already?"

She turned, recognizing him immediately. Caleb stood a few feet away, wiping his hands on his jeans.

"Not lost," she corrected thoughtfully. "Just...strategizing."

"The 'map' phase. That's progress."

"Is it?"

"Definitely. Day one was the 'don't fall in the water' phase."

She laughed. "I suppose that is progress."

"What are you looking for?"

She indicated toward the map. "The Bayview Inn. My sister wants photos of everything."

"You're close. Follow the shoreline. Big impressive white building. Rocking chairs on the porch."

"That sounds exactly like what I pictured."

"Mahone Bay tends to live up to its reputation."

There was a pause. Comfortable. Easy.

"Are you always rescuing newcomers?" she asked, squinting slightly against the glare of the sun.

"Only the ones who look like they might actually stay." He paused. "You planning to?"

She surprised herself by answering honestly. "I think so."

Something shifted in his expression—acknowledgment, maybe. Understanding.

"Well," he said, clearing his throat, "I should get back to work."

"Of course. Thank you. For...last time. And today."

"You're welcome."

As she walked away, he watched her again. This time, he didn't bother pretending it was merely out of concern.

• • • •

MARISSA FOLLOWED THE shoreline path, her heart light and free, certainly more so than it had been when she first arrived. She took in the town around her in its small details: a porch swing moving gently in the breeze; a window display of handmade candles; a chalkboard sign outside a shop reading *Today's mood: hot cocoa and kindness.*

The Bayview Inn appeared exactly as Caleb had intimated—stately and welcoming, its wrap-around porch lined with white rocking chairs and a few hanging lanterns that looked charming even in daylight. Lavender planters perched near the steps, the faint scent rising on the breeze.

Marissa lifted her phone to take photos for her sister and nearly collided with a woman carrying a basket of folded linens.

"Oh—sorry," Marissa blurted, stepping back quickly.

The woman steadied the basket with a practiced motion and smiled. She appeared to be around Marissa's age, with dark hair pulled into a low ponytail and an expression that portrayed her as both capable and kind.

"No harm done," she said. "First time up the steps? They have a way of surprising people."

Marissa laughed, relief loosening her shoulders. "I guess there's no denying it now, is there?"

"Not a chance," the woman teased gently. "I'm Tessa."

"Marissa."

"Tessa O'Donnell," she added, shifting the basket. "I run the Bayview. Or I try to, most days."

Marissa glanced at the porch and the sparkling windows, the airy warmth of the place obvious. "It's beautiful."

"Thank you." Tessa's smile softened. "We try to make it feel like one has been expected."

Marissa's throat tightened at the sentimental expression. "That's...a lovely way to put it."

Tessa nodded as if she understood what Marissa hadn't said out loud. "Are you staying here?"

"No, I'm renting a little place near the harbor. I got here a few days ago."

"Then, welcome," Tessa said simply. "If you need anything—extra blankets, directions, a place to sit where you can hear the water without thinking too hard—come by."

Marissa smiled, startled by the sincerity. "Thank you."

Tessa adjusted the basket again and gave her a quick knowing look. "Also—if you're taking photos for someone back home, make sure you get the lanterns at dusk. The porch looks like it came right out of a fairytale."

Marissa's chest warmed. "I will."

As Tessa disappeared inside, Marissa remained on the porch for a moment longer, letting the wind brush her cheeks and the word *welcome* settle into her soul.

She took a few photos, smiling contentedly as she sent them to her sister.

You look like you found something, her sister replied.

Marissa typed slowly.

Maybe I did.

She lowered her phone and stared at the water. Mahone Bay no longer felt like a risk. It felt like a warm invitation.

• • • •

BY THE FOURTH MORNING, Marissa had developed what almost resembled a routine. Wake with the gulls. Dress in clothes that felt far too clean for a town so salt-worn. Walk to the harbor. Watch the boats.

And then—because she'd done it once and the pattern felt easy and comfortable—head to the Harborlight Café.

The bell chimed in greeting as she stepped inside. Sophie looked up from behind the counter and smiled with the easy recognition and expectation of someone who'd already assimilated Marissa's visits into her morning schedule.

"Back again," Sophie remarked rhetorically.

"The coffee's good," Marissa responded.

"The coffee's fine. It's the company you're after."

Marissa laughed, surprised at Sophie's insight and ability to pinpoint the truth.

She ordered the same thing as the previous day—coffee and a blueberry scone—and chose the same window seat with a view of the marina. The repetition grounded her. In the city, routine had implied obligation. In Mahone Bay, it felt like choice.

The café was busier than on previous days. A cluster of women sat at a corner table, their conversation animated but warm. An older man relaxed by the fireplace and leisurely read a newspaper, his coffee cup refilled twice by Sophie without him having to ask. A younger couple shared a muffin, their fingers intertwined on the tabletop.

Marissa sipped her coffee and listened to the interactions around her.

"—and then she said she'd bring the casserole, but you know Eleanor, she'll forget—"

"—needs help with the deck railing before winter really sets in—"

"—Saturday market's coming up, we should get there early for Eliza's bread—"

The conversations didn't so much as overlap as they wove together into something less like separate exchanges and more like a single ongoing dialogue between the townsfolk.

A woman emerged from the kitchen—older, with gray hair twisted into a loose bun and an air of quiet authority. She wiped a hand on her apron and surveyed the room with the practiced eye of someone who caught everything.

Her gaze landed on Marissa.

For a moment, Marissa felt exposed—seen in the sense that made her want to look away. But the woman's expression wasn't unkind. Just...assessing.

She walked over, carrying a small plate with a fresh cinnamon roll that looked like it had just come out of the oven, still steaming.

"You're new," she said, setting the plate down on Marissa's table.

"Yes. I'm Marissa."

"Isla Sullivan. I own this place." She nodded toward the plate. "On the house. We feed newcomers until they stop looking so nervous."

Marissa blinked. "I'm not—"

"You are," Isla asserted, not unkindly. "But you're getting better. Yesterday, you looked like you might bolt. Today, you just look like you're thinking about it."

A surprised laugh escaped Marissa's throat. "That's accurate."

"Most people don't make it past three days if they're not serious about staying," Isla continued. "The ones who are just passing through get bored by day two. You're still here."

"I'm still deciding," Marissa admitted.

Isla studied her a moment longer, then nodded once as if Marissa had passed some invisible test. "Take your time. The town's not going anywhere."

She returned to the kitchen, leaving Marissa with the cinnamon roll and a strange, unfamiliar feeling in her chest.

The women at the corner table were organizing something—collecting names, dividing tasks. One of them noticed Marissa watching and smiled.

"Fundraiser for the community center," she explained in an amicable timbre. "Happens every March. You should come."

"I—I'm not sure I'll still be here," Marissa answered frankly.

"Well," the woman said easily, "if you are, you're welcome."

Not *you should*. Not *you must*. Just *you're welcome*.

Marissa finished her coffee slowly, allowing both the brew's warmth and that of the café to settle into her bones. Outside, the harbor glittered in morning light. A fishing boat chugged past, hungry gulls trailing behind it like ducklings.

Marissa reflected on city life—how she'd moved through crowds of people without ever feeling seen. On meetings where her presence was expected but her voice was optional, if not preferably suppressed. On the apartment where she'd lived for three years without learning any of her neighbors' names.

In the Bay, what she had affectionately come to call Mahone Bay, someone gave her a cinnamon roll just because she looked nervous.

It was such a small gesture, yet it felt enormous.

When she finally stood to leave, Sophie called out from behind the counter. "See you tomorrow?"

This time, Marissa didn't hesitate. "Yes."

Outside, the cool air brushed her cheeks. She walked slowly back toward her rental, taking the long route past the marina, the bookstore, the small shops with their hand-painted signs.

She wasn't ready to call the Bay home yet.

But she was ready to stop pretending it was only temporary.

Chapter Three

By her fifth morning in Mahone Bay, Marissa had stopped cataloging every moment like evidence. Some things were beginning to feel familiar—the walk to the harbor, the way Sophie greeted her at the café, the particular slant of morning's light on the water. And somehow, that made them feel more authentic.

She stood in line at the Harborlight Café, already knowing what she was going to order and already recognizing half the faces around her. People greeted one another by name, asked after families, paused to listen instead of speaking over one another.

When she reached the counter, Sophie looked up and grinned. "You're officially becoming a regular."

Marissa laughed softly. The words startled her more than they should have. A few days earlier, she had been anonymous. Now, she was expected, noticed. "Is there a ceremony for that?"

"Coffee on the house the tenth time you forget your wallet."

"I'll aim for that milestone."

She ordered her usual and hesitated, fingers tightening slightly around her purse strap. "Sophie...can I ask you something?"

"Always."

"Do you ever need help here? Not permanently, necessarily. Just...I'd like to be useful. And I'd like to meet people in a way that isn't just passing through."

Sophie's smile softened into one of warmth and thoughtfulness. "That's a brave thing to ask."

"It doesn't feel brave," Marissa admitted. "It feels like stepping into something without knowing where my footing is—like the loose board at the marina I encountered the other day and nearly went for a swim!"

"Feeling out of one's depth is usually how belonging starts," Sophie said sagely. "We're actually short-handed with Sarah on maternity leave. Let me talk to Isla—she's the owner. But I'm sure she'll say yes."

Marissa's chest loosened as she let out her breath. "Thank you."

She took her coffee and stepped outside, the morning air cool and crisp. Asking had taken more courage than she wanted to admit.

She found herself following her feet toward the marina, the path already familiar. And there he was.

Caleb stood bent forward near the old boat shed, sleeves rolled up, sanding a long piece of wood with slow, careful strokes. Sawdust clung to his hands and the hem of his hoodie. He stilled momentarily, and as the sunlight caught in his dark hair, he blended in as part of the landscape—steady and rooted.

Marissa hesitated, not wanting to interrupt.

He looked up as he sensed her presence. "Good morning, Marissa."

It still surprised her how easily her name rolled off his tongue in his unhurried cadence. "Good morning. I hope I'm not in the way."

"Not at all." He set the sandpaper down. "What brings you down here today?"

"I asked about helping at the café," she said. "They might let me."

"They'd be smart to," he replied with a grin.

She smiled, warmth blooming in her chest. "What are you working on?"

"Bookshelf. For The Tides."

"The bookstore? I walked past it yesterday—it looked very enticing with the comfy corner couches to sit and read all those books."

"That's Lila's doing. She says people need comfort to read books almost as much as books need comfort to feel brave enough to call to a reader to be opened."

Marissa loved that. "Are you building a reading nook?"

"Installing one. Want to help?"

The offer surprised her. "Me?"

"Only if you want to. It's not complicated. Just heavier than it looks."

A week earlier, she would have automatically said no. She set her coffee on the bench. "I can handle heavy."

They lifted the board together, their hands brushing once, briefly. The contact was accidental, but it sent a quiet awareness through her that lingered long after they adjusted their grip.

"You good?" he asked.

"Yes," she said, a little too quickly. Then more honestly, "I think so."

They carried the shelf to The Tides together, navigating the narrow street carefully in synchrony.

Inside the bookstore, the warm air was dusted with the scent of paper and cedar. A woman with auburn hair looked up from behind the counter.

"Caleb! You're early."

"I brought help," he stated good-naturedly.

Lila's eyes flicked to Marissa with immediate interest. "You must be new. I'm Lila."

"Marissa. I just arrived a few days ago."

They worked side by side, fitting the shelf into place. It took coordination and patience. At one point, Marissa misjudged the angle and bumped into Caleb's shoulder.

"Sorry."

"Don't be. We're learning," he said kindly.

The word settled warmly between them.

Once the shelf was secure, Lila stepped back and clasped her hands. "It's perfect."

They stood admiring their work for a moment, and Lila smiled warmly at both of them before returning to help a customer who'd just entered.

Marissa smiled, a quiet pride filling her. "Something beautiful to hold stories."

"Indeed," Caleb echoed.

Outside the bookstore, the sun was now higher.

Caleb glanced at Marissa. "Favorite story?"

The question startled her. "That's...dangerous territory."

"Only if you don't answer."

She thought for a moment. "I like stories where people find their way home in unexpected ways."

He nodded slowly. "That sounds like you."

She met his gaze, surprised by how seen she felt.

"What about you?"

"Stories where people choose to stay," he said simply.

Her heart tightened in response to the pure honesty in his voice.

They left the bookstore together, the sun overhead and the street alive with townsfolk and quiet hellos.

"You don't usually ask for help, do you?" Marissa asked thoughtfully.

"No."

"Why me?"

"Because you're not wearing a façade or trying to impress anyone," he replied. "You're authentic and real."

Her breath caught. "That might be the nicest thing anyone's ever said to me."

"It's the truth."

They walked back toward the marina, an easy silence settling between them.

Later that afternoon, Marissa returned to her rental and had the strange, steady feeling that she was no longer learning the ropes of Mahone Bay like a visitor.

She was beginning to learn them like someone who intended to stay.

Chapter Four

The café bell no longer registered enough in her mind to make her pause on the threshold like someone hesitantly entering another's abode. By her seventh morning in Mahone Bay, the jingle had started to represent possibility, community, and belonging rather than interruption, loneliness, and isolation.

Sophie had called the evening before. "Isla says yes. Can you start tomorrow? Seven o'clock?"

Marissa had said yes before her nerves could trip her up.

Now, at six fifty-five, she stood outside the Harborlight Café, watching her breath mist in the cool morning air. She could see movement through the window—Sophie arranging mugs, someone in the back kitchen sliding trays into the oven.

She pushed the door open.

The warmth hit her immediately, along with the tantalizing scent of fresh bread and brewing coffee. Sophie looked up and grinned.

"You're early. I like that." She held out an apron. "Ready?"

Marissa accepted it like it was something precious, an honor to don. "I think so."

Isla emerged from the back, sleeves rolled up, gray hair twisted into a loose bun. Marissa immediately remembered the steaming cinnamon roll the kind woman had given her on the house a few days earlier.

"Good morning, Marissa. Sophie tells me you offered to help."

"Yes. I hope that wasn't strange or impolite."

"Strange or impolite?" Isla smiled faintly. "It was thoughtful. And brave. Can you pour coffee and carry plates without dropping them?"

"I can try," Marissa replied, half laughing.

"That's all anyone ever does here. The job's yours if you want it—three mornings a week to start, minimum wage plus tips. We'll do the paperwork this afternoon."

The words settled over Marissa like a soft blanket on a cold winter's eve. Comfortable. Homey. Warm. "Thank you."

"Don't thank me yet. Wait until after the breakfast rush," Isla quipped with a snort.

The first few moments were awkward. Marissa fumbled with the coffee pot, nearly collided with Sophie twice, and forgot which table had ordered what.

"You're doing fine," Sophie whispered.

"I feel like I'm in the way and more trouble than help."

"You're learning. Be kind to yourself."

Gradually, Marissa settled into a rhythm. Pour. Smile. Carry. Listen. Remember a name. Ask a question. Move aside when someone needed space.

A man with silver hair winked at her. "You're new."

"Yes."

"Good. Keeps the rest of us honest."

She laughed, surprised at the ease with which it bubbled from deep in her soul.

Another woman asked where Marissa was from. A young couple asked if she planned to stay. Each answer felt like another brick laid in cementing her decision to stay in the Bay.

"You're doing great," Sophie murmured again.

Marissa realized she meant it.

The café emptied slowly after the breakfast rush, the last few customers lingering over second, third, or even fourth cups of coffee and quiet conversation. Sophie wiped down tables while Isla tallied receipts at the register.

"Marissa," Isla called. "Do you have a few minutes before you go?"

Marissa's stomach fluttered with sudden nervousness. Had she done something wrong? Forgotten something important?

She followed Isla into the tiny office behind the kitchen—barely more than a closet with a desk, filing cabinet, and a corkboard covered in pinned schedules and receipts. Isla pulled out a folder and set it on the desk.

"Paperwork," she said in explanation. "I should've done this before your shift, but mornings get away from me."

"Oh," Marissa said, relief coursing through her. "Of course."

Isla slid a tax form across the desk, then an employee information sheet. "Standard stuff. The pay is minimum wage plus tips—not much, but it's honest work. You'll get paid every two weeks."

Marissa filled out the forms carefully, her handwriting neat and small. When she reached the line for permanent address, her pen hovered.

The rental was temporary. Month-to-month. She could write that address, but it felt dishonest somehow—like claiming something she hadn't yet earned.

"You can use the rental address for now," Isla said as if reading her mind. "You can always update it later when things change."

When. Not *if*.

Marissa penned the address.

"Sarah—the woman whose shifts you're covering—had her baby two weeks ago," Isla informed Marissa, leaning back in her chair. "Beautiful little girl. Third child. She'll be home for at least three months, maybe longer. Which means if you're planning to stay, the job is yours for as long as you want it."

"I..." Marissa paused. "I'm planning to stay."

The words surprised her even as she said them out loud. But they felt true.

Isla smiled—not the polite smile she'd given on their first meeting but something warmer. "Good. The café runs on people who care, not just people who show up. You care. I can tell."

"How so?" Marissa asked.

"The way you arranged those scones this morning. Like they mattered. Like customers would notice." Isla stood, gathering the papers.

"In the city, nobody notices that kind of thing. Here, everything small matters because we're a small community. We take care of what we have."

Marissa felt her throat tighten. "I want to learn how to do that."

"You already are," Isla said with a nod.

When Marissa stepped out of the office, Sophie was waiting with her jacket and a small paper bag.

"Day-old croissants," Sophie said, pressing the bag into Marissa's hands. "Another café perk. We never waste food—it either gets eaten by staff or donated. You're staff now."

Staff. The word anchored Marissa.

She walked out of the café with the bag of croissants and the weight of the forms she'd filled out—proof that she was building something in the Bay. Not just visiting. Not just hiding.

Building.

She stopped at the small general store on the way home and bought a canvas tote bag with a lighthouse printed on it. Something local. Something that said *I live here*, not *I'm passing through*.

The woman at the register smiled. "New in town?"

"Yes," Marissa said. "But I'm staying."

And for the first time, she didn't add any qualifiers.

• • • •

CALEB NOTICED THE DIFFERENCE the second he set foot in the café.

Marissa moved behind the counter with careful confidence, apron tied at her waist, hair pulled back loosely. She didn't look like someone awkwardly navigating a new space. She looked like someone comfortable and well-acquainted.

The sight stirred something unfamiliar in his chest.

He ordered coffee and lingered longer than necessary.

"You look busy," he commented lazily as he took a sip of coffee.

She turned, eyes lighting when she saw him. "I am. In the best way."

"Looks like you've been put to work."

"I got hired, actually," she corrected, a hint of pride in her voice. "There's a difference."

He smiled. "That sounds like you."

Their eyes held for a moment longer than the casual conversation required.

"So," he pressed gently, "how does it feel?"

She considered her answer. "Like I'm useful. But also...like I'm seen."

Her refreshing honesty stilled something in him. "You are."

• • • •

LATER THAT AFTERNOON, after her shift had ended and she was sauntering homeward, Marissa came across Caleb sitting on a bench near the marina, sketching something in a small notebook.

"You draw?" she asked.

He looked up, not startled. "Boat designs, mostly. Helps me think."

"Can I sit?"

"Please."

She settled beside him, not too close, not too far. They took in the ocean's mesmerizing motion in comfortable silence.

"I'm afraid of getting attached too quickly," she said finally.

He didn't dismiss her vulnerable confession. "Why?"

"Because I don't know how to tell the difference between belonging and depending."

He studied her thoughtfully. "Depending means you stop standing on your own. Belonging means you choose where you stand."

Her breath caught. "That's...helpful."

"Also true."

She pulled out her own sketchbook—the one she'd been carrying since the city. "I draw sometimes, too. Places, mostly. When I'm trying to put into a picture the reflections and emotions they evoke in me."

"Have you drawn Mahone Bay yet?"

“Pieces of it.” She showed him a quick sketch of the harbor at dawn, the lighthouse barely visible through morning mist.

“That’s good,” he complimented quietly.

“It’s unfinished.”

“So is belonging.”

They sat together as the afternoon softened, the conversation settling into something deeper than words.

“I should go,” she said eventually, though she didn’t move right away.

“See you tomorrow?”

“Yes,” she said without hesitation. And meant it.

Chapter Five

Nearly two weeks in, Marissa had started to recognize the way Mahone Bay shifted its moods. Sun meant ease. Fog meant quiet. Rain meant pause.

She had just stepped out of The Tides—having spent an hour browsing while Lila recommended books—when the first drops hit. Within seconds, it thickened into a steady curtain, blurring the harbor into watercolor shapes. She was already halfway to the harbor when the rain came pouring down, so she hurried toward the old boat shed where she knew there was shelter.

It smelled faintly of varnish and old wood, with a trace of salt from the harbor. The rain pounded a steady rhythm on the tin roof.

"You beat me to it."

She turned. Caleb stood just inside the entrance, shaking rain from his jacket.

"I had a head start," she said with a chuckle.

"Looks like we're both waiting it out."

She leaned against the wooden wall. "This place feels safe."

Caleb nodded. "It's weathered a lot of storms."

The rain intensified, drumming against the roof and blotting out all other sense of sound or sight; the rest of the world felt very far away.

"Can I ask you something?" Marissa said, having to raise her voice to compete with the deluge.

"Always."

"Why are you so patient and kind to me?"

He didn't answer without first mulling over his answer. She watched him consider it.

"Because you're without airs, not pretending you already know how everything works 'round here or that you have all the big-city answers. You're open to learning about the people, places, and practices here," he said finally.

Her chest tightened. "And you? Why do you appear guarded?"

He released a slow breath. "Because people don't always stay. And it's easier to prepare for them leaving than to hope for them staying."

She nodded. "You're afraid people will disappear."

"Yes."

"And you're afraid I will."

The truth flickered across his face. "I'm trying not to make that your burden."

She stepped closer, not touching him but close enough that their presence felt shared. "I don't want to become something you rely on in a way that traps either of us. But I also don't want to pretend this isn't real or doesn't matter."

"What does it feel like to you?"

"Like we're walking beside each other. Not holding each other up. Just...choosing the same direction and affording each other companionship along the way."

He regarded her with quiet respect. "Yeah. That's exactly it."

Marissa shifted slightly, her shoulder brushing his. The contact was unintentional, but neither moved away.

When the rain eased to a light spatter, they stepped out into the fresh air together. The harbor smelled clean, renewed.

At the fork in the path, Marissa stopped.

"This was important," she said.

"It was."

As they walked back along the wet dock, the air smelled untainted and fresh. Rain always did that—washed away the accumulated filth and grime and left everything sharper, brighter, clearer. Rainwater dripped from the edges of boat canopies. Puddles reflected the sky in fractured pieces of blue and gray.

Caleb stopped, tilting his head toward the harbor. "Look."

Marissa followed his gaze. A rainbow arced over the water, faint but unmistakable—one end disappearing into the mist near the far shore, the other dissolving somewhere above the lighthouse.

"I've never seen one over the bay before," he murmured. "At least not in years."

They stood drinking in the sight together, neither speaking, as if words might break whatever fragile magic was holding it in place.

The rainbow faded slowly, bleeding back into the clouds until only the memory of color remained.

"Marissa! Caleb!"

They turned as one. Sophie was hurrying toward them, umbrella in hand, even though the rain had now stopped. She was laughing.

"I saw you two caught in the storm from the café window," she said, slightly breathless. "I was about to bring you an umbrella, but you looked like you'd already made peace with being soaked."

Caleb smiled. "We found shelter."

"I'll bet you did," Sophie replied, her eyes twinkling with something Marissa couldn't quite discern. Not an assumption. Just...noticing. "Well, don't catch a cold. Both of you."

She headed back toward the café, still smiling to herself.

Marissa glanced at Caleb. "Does the whole town—?"

"Notice things?" he finished. "Yes. It's one of the advantages and challenges of living here. Privacy is relative."

"And you're okay with that?"

He paused to consider. "I've learned that being seen isn't the same as being judged. Here, people see you because they care, not because they're keeping score."

The distinction settled into Marissa's soul like something she'd been looking for without knowing its name.

They stood a moment more, balanced between patience and possibility, before going their separate ways.

Chapter Six

Two and a half weeks after arriving in Mahone Bay, tentative routines had cemented and become the norm. Marissa was standing in the small grocery store, the kind with narrow aisles and handwritten price tags, holding a basket that contained bread, apples, a jar of local honey, and a bundle of fresh rosemary tied with twine. The kind of items one bought when one expected to be in a place long enough to use them.

This isn't temporary anymore.

The thought didn't come with panic but with calm.

She wasn't visiting Mahone Bay. She was living in it.

A woman ahead of her in line turned and smiled. "You haven't been here long, have you?"

Marissa shook her head. "Just a few weeks."

"Well, welcome. You picked a good season to arrive."

After paying, Marissa took the long way home, passing three shops whose owners knew her by name. By the time she reached the shoreline path, the sentiment had reshaped itself: *I want this. And I'm afraid because I want this.*

• • • •

SHE FOUND CALEB NEAR the bench by the lighthouse later that afternoon.

"Everything okay?" he asked.

She nodded. "Just thinking."

"That usually means something important."

She rested her hands on the back of the bench and stared out at the water. "I don't think I can pretend this is temporary anymore," she shared.

He didn't interrupt.

"I used to treat new places like waiting rooms," she continued. "Somewhere to sit until my real life started again. But this..." She gestured toward the harbor. "This feels like my life."

"And that scares you."

"Yes."

"Why?"

"Because staying means choosing. And choosing means trusting something enough to let it matter." She paused and looked at the panoramic ocean view. "Does it always feel this exposed?"

"Yes," he said simply. "That's how you know it's real."

She laughed softly. "I wish there were instructions."

"Mahone Bay doesn't come with those."

They shared a small smile.

"I want to stay," she whispered. "It scares me."

Caleb felt the warmth in her words like sunlight breaking through fog. Part of him wanted to believe them without question. But another part of him remembered the last time someone had said they were staying—and how quickly that changed. He pushed the thought aside, but it lingered, reminding him that trust was still a choice.

They stood in silence, the water shifting gently beside them.

• • • •

THAT EVENING, CALEB sat on his porch long after the sky had relinquished its color palette and clothed itself in darkness, Marissa's words echoing in his mind.

I want to stay.

He had spent years constantly in the cycle of preparing himself for departure.

People came, people left. The harbor stayed. That had been his rule.

But Marissa wasn't drifting. She was choosing.

And that made everything different.

Chapter Seven

A month in, Mahone Bay no longer greeted Marissa like a stranger. The morning arrived wrapped in fog, rolling in from the harbor like a slow breath, softening the edges of everything it touched. Boats became shadows. The water turned to pale glass. Even the houses hugging the shoreline serenely held their secrets.

Marissa stood at the end of the dock, her jacket pulled close, watching the morning mist curl around the evenly spaced pilings. The world felt frozen in time, suspended.

She hadn't slept much. Not because she was restless but because her thoughts had circled quietly all night, returning again and again to the same truth.

She wasn't visiting Mahone Bay anymore. She was choosing to put down roots and open her heart and soul.

Footsteps sounded behind her, familiar and unhurried.

"I thought I might find you here," Caleb said, his voice magnified by the crisp air.

She turned, smiling softly. "I wanted to see the town before it woke up completely."

"Fog mornings do that," he commented. "They slow everything down. Instead of the town waking up like a bird at first light, it's more like a flower that opens slowly as the sun rises."

"I like it."

They sauntered together toward the end of the dock. She rested her hands on the railing, and after a moment, he mirrored her posture beside her.

"I'm not leaving," she said quietly.

"You're sure?"

"Yes." She turned to meet his eyes. "I want to build a life here."

His expression was open, one of relief, vulnerability, hope. "That's a brave thing to say out loud."

"I don't want to only be considered brave for walking away," she replied. "I want to be considered courageous for staying."

He nodded slowly. "I already see you as such."

The cocoon of fog began to thin, opening to reveal faint outlines of the boats and the shoreline as though emerging like a beautiful butterfly after a wintry metamorphosis.

"There's something I need to tell you," he said after a moment. "I didn't expect to come to care about you. I told myself I shouldn't, wouldn't. But you never acted like someone passing through..."

Her breath caught. "Caleb..."

"I don't need promises," he added gently. "I just need honesty."

She took a step closer, the space between them suddenly charged. "Then I'll be honest. I don't know exactly what this is yet. But I know it matters. And I don't want to pretend it doesn't."

A relieved smile touched his lips. "That's all I was hoping for."

She reached for his hand, gentle and unhurried, and when their fingers touched, it felt like a tangible confirmation of what she had described—not a spark but a warmth. A recognition.

Caleb's thumb brushed lightly across her knuckles. "Is this okay?"

She nodded, her voice barely a whisper. "More than okay."

They stayed that way for a long moment, watching as the last of the fog cocoon retracted and the harbor appeared fully. Boats took on full shape. The sea turned liquid blue again.

For Marissa, the shared moment felt quietly monumental.

Later, they walked back toward town side by side.

"This doesn't have to be complicated," she said. "We don't have to define everything today."

"I like that," he answered. "We'll let it grow."

At the Harborlight Café, Sophie spotted them through the window and quirked an eyebrow playfully. Marissa felt a blush rise, but she didn't avert her gaze. For once, she didn't want to conceal something that felt so honest and good.

Caleb squeezed her hand once before letting go. "I'll see you later?"

"Yes," she said with conviction. "I'd like that."

As he walked away, Marissa savored the moment, her heart steady and full.

She wasn't standing at the edge of something unknown anymore. She was standing inside her choice, knowing and being known.

• • • •

THAT EVENING, SHE WALKED down to the marina again, alone this time. The harbor lights were just beginning to glow in dusk's shadow, one by one, reflecting softly across the water. Gold rippled against blue. Warmth against calm.

She leaned against the railing and watched them, thinking of how every light was someone's decision to stay awake a little longer. To tend to something or someone. To care.

Some stories didn't begin with grand declarations. Some began with a quiet promise to remain.

Chapter Eight

The Saturday market felt like the town had decided to harness all its friendliness into one place for an extravaganza. Marissa slowed at the edge of the square, breathing in the mingled aromas of fresh bread, citrus, and something warm and spiced. Stalls with wares lined the walkway in neat rows—local honey, knitted scarves, jars of jam, handmade soaps stacked like pastel bricks. Someone played a guitar near the fountain, the melody soft and familiar even though she didn't recognize it.

She told herself she was there for something simple. A basket. Flowers for her kitchen table. Maybe another jar of honey.

But truthfully, she was there to test the waters of her belonging, to dip her toe in and see whether the water was warm, welcoming, inviting—or if it was cold, censoring, and uncaring.

Sophie had described it as "the easiest way to meet the town," which sounded like something only a local would say. In Marissa's experience, meeting people had never been easy. It had always required a version of herself that performed—polished, functional, agreeable. The version that didn't show all of her layers, only the exterior.

In Mahone Bay, the town seemed to notice one's presence before one had even decided how to introduce oneself.

"Marissa!"

Sophie waved from a stall stacked with small bouquets packaged in brown paper.

"You came," Sophie said as Marissa approached.

"I did," Marissa replied, smiling. "I'm trying to be brave."

Sophie leaned in, lowering her voice. "The key is to pretend you already belong. Your confidence will be convincing."

Marissa laughed. "That sounds illegal."

"Only if you refuse the muffins someone offers you."

Sophie pressed a small bouquet into Marissa's hands—white daisies and greenery. "I got these for your table," she declared.

Marissa's eyes widened. "Sophie—"

"Don't fight it," Sophie insisted. "Market rule: you don't leave empty-handed."

"Thank you."

Sophie gestured to the next stall, where a kind-looking woman arranged loaves of bread with careful attention.

"That's Eliza Sullivan," Sophie murmured. "Isla's sister. She lives up in Cape Breton, but she comes down every other month to sell her sourdough."

Eliza looked up and smiled. "Morning, Sophie."

"Morning," Sophie replied brightly. "Eliza, this is Marissa. "She's helping us at Harborlight now."

Marissa blinked at the phrasing.

Helping us. Not *passing through*.

Eliza's smile widened. "Welcome. You picked a good place to land."

The words felt less like courtesy and more like confirmation.

"Thank you," Marissa said. "Everyone keeps saying that."

"Because it's true," Eliza replied with a wise timbre to her voice.

Sophie wandered off, and Marissa drifted between stalls of preserves, ceramics, and handmade scarves. She listened more than she spoke, absorbing the rhythm of conversation and interaction.

And then she heard it.

"Oh, you're the one from the city."

The voice was too loud to be unintentional. Marissa turned and found a woman with perfectly coiffed hair and a smile that didn't reach her eyes.

"I—sorry?" Marissa replied.

The woman nodded brusquely. "I'm Darlene. You're helping at Harborlight, aren't you? I heard Isla brought someone in."

Marissa's stomach dipped in panic and trepidation. "I...I offered. They h...hired me."

Darlene's smile tightened perceptibly. "Oh. Well. That's...enthusiastic."

Marissa fought the old instinct to shrink. "I like it there," she asserted, feeling like a little kitten trying to be a lion. "It feels like community."

Darlene tilted her head. "Community's wonderful. It's just...some people try to step into it too quickly. It takes time to become—*known*."

The word cut through her newfound bravado with jagged edges.

"I'm not asking to be known in a vacuum," Marissa said, steadying her voice. "I want to participate, to get to know the town's people, and to find ways and for them to get to know me." The kitten felt more like a lion this time.

Darlene's brows lifted. "How modern."

Someone appeared beside Marissa.

Caleb.

He didn't look at Darlene at first. He looked at Marissa, his gaze steady, as if checking whether she was okay.

"You found the market," he said, his eyes silently encouraging her that all was well.

"I did," she replied, the relief loosening the tightness the exchange with Darlene had wrought in her chest.

Caleb then turned to Darlene, polite but resolute. "Morning, Darlene."

"Caleb," she gushed, her voice suddenly sweeter and her demeanor congenial. "I didn't realize you were—"

"I'm with Marissa," Caleb said simply.

Not possessive. Just clear.

Darlene blinked, recalculating. "Oh. Well. Enjoy." She offered one last tight smile and drifted away.

Marissa exhaled slowly.

Caleb nodded toward the bouquet in her hands. "Those suit you."

"Sophie forced them on me."

"Sounds like Sophie."

Marissa hesitated, then said quietly, "Thank you. For stepping in."

"You didn't need rescuing."

"Maybe," she agreed. "But I needed someone to bolster my bravado and make it clear I'm not alone."

His gaze held hers. "You're not."

A gust of wind moved across the square as the market continued around them.

They walked together for a while after that—past the jam stall, past the pottery table, past the guitarist. People nodded to Marissa now. Not because she was new but because she was familiar.

Belonging didn't mean everyone welcomed you.

It meant the people that counted did—and you stopped apologizing for it.

They found a small table near the market's edge, where someone had set up a coffee cart. Caleb bought them both cups—dark roast, steam rising in the cool morning air—and they sat watching the flow of people around them.

"Does it bother you?" Marissa asked after a moment. "What you overheard Darlene saying to me?"

Caleb shook his head. "Every town has a Darlene. Someone who thinks belonging is something you inherit or buy instead of something you build. She doesn't define this place."

"But she's part of it."

"So are fifty other people who've gone out of their way to make you feel welcome." He gestured toward the market. "Look around. Really look."

Marissa obeyed. She saw Eliza wrapping a loaf of bread for an elderly man, adding an extra roll with a wink. She spotted Sophie laughing with a vendor selling handmade scarves. A mother was chasing a toddler between the stalls while three different people called out amused cheers.

"Community isn't perfect," Caleb continued. "It's just people choosing to show up for each other more often than not. Darlene is one voice. You've got a whole chorus saying something different."

A small girl—maybe five or six—ran up to their table, breathless and grinning. "Caleb! Are you still helping with the winter carnival?"

He smiled. "Wouldn't miss it, Emma."

"Good! Dad says you're building the ice rink frame." She noticed Marissa and tilted her head with open curiosity. "Are you Caleb's girlfriend?"

"Emma," Caleb chided, laughing. "Personal questions."

"Mom says personal questions are how you make friends," Emma replied matter-of-factly.

Marissa bit back a smile. "I'm Marissa. I'm new in town."

"Oh! You work at the café! Mom says you make the best coffee." Emma beamed at her. "You should help with the carnival, too. Everyone helps. It's fun."

Before Marissa could answer, Emma's father called her name from across the market. She waved and darted off, leaving Marissa and Caleb in her wake.

"Winter carnival?" Marissa asked.

"February tradition. Ice skating, hot chocolate, sledding if there's enough snow. The whole town shows up—it's chaotic and wonderful."

"You build the ice rink?"

"Help build it. It's a community effort."

The invitation hung between them—not just to an event but to another layer of belonging. To being part of the rhythm of the place.

"I'd like to help," she said.

An older woman stopped by their table, someone Marissa had served at the café but whose name she couldn't quite recall. "Marissa, dear. I just wanted to say thank you for remembering my tea preference yesterday. It's the little things, the details, that matter when you get to my age."

"Of course, Mrs. Patterson," Marissa said kindly, the name coming to her suddenly.

The woman smiled and moved on.

Caleb raised his eyebrows. "You remembered her name."

"She comes in every Thursday. Earl Grey, extra hot, splash of milk."

"That's what I mean," he said quietly. "You're not just working there. You're paying attention. You're part of it."

Marissa looked around the market again—at the people who'd greeted her, who'd smiled, who'd invited her to help with carnivals and welcomed her presence. Darlene's words felt powerless now. One sour note in a much larger song.

"I am, aren't I?" she said, almost to herself.

"Yeah," Caleb said. "You are."

Epilogue

The fragrant aromas of cinnamon and butter filled the Harborlight Café before sunrise. Six weeks in Mahone Bay, Marissa no longer felt like a passing patron of the café; she felt like a part of the bricks and mortar that held it all together.

Isla Sullivan bustled through the kitchen with quiet authority, sliding trays into the oven and checking timers. The espresso machine bubbled and hissed. Sophie wiped down tables, humming under her breath. Outside, the harbor was still ensconced in night.

Marissa tied her apron and paused for a moment behind the counter, drinking in the now familiar and centering sounds around her.

The early rush had its own music: mugs clinking, chair legs scraping gently, a low murmur of voices, the bell chiming as the first regulars stepped inside.

She lifted the tongs and arranged the first batch of blueberry-lemon scones in the display case; her movements felt natural with the ease of someone who respected the space she'd been trusted with.

"You ready?" Sophie asked.

Marissa smiled. "I think I am."

The bell tinkled. Caleb stepped inside, brushing remnants of the cold from his jacket. His gaze found Marissa almost immediately—not urgently but with a quiet certainty.

"Morning," he said.

"Morning," Marissa answered, warmth rising into her cheeks.

He ordered coffee and lingered at the counter. Isla glanced at Marissa with a knowing look before disappearing into the back.

"You look settled," Caleb said softly.

Marissa considered the word. "I am. I feel present. That's new for me."

He smiled in a way that made her heart squeeze. "It suits you."

Their fingers brushed when she handed him his mug.

"I'll walk you down to the marina after the rush," he said.

"I'd like that."

The café filled slowly, then steadily. Marissa moved with confidence—pouring coffee, clearing plates, answering questions. She knew who would come in first. Who liked extra cream. Which table creaked.

In the city, she had been valued for being useful. In Mahone Bay, she was known.

The bell chimed again.

A woman stepped inside, brushing the cold from her coat, her expression both tired and hopeful. Marissa recognized her from one of Sophie's previous narratives and by the way Isla straightened just a little.

"Maren," Isla said softly from the kitchen doorway.

Maren's smile wavered, then steadied. "Hi, Aunt Isla."

They embraced briefly with the tenderness of people who had missed one another.

Marissa approached with a small smile and a mug of coffee. "Welcome to Harborlight."

Maren looked at her with surprise, then relief. "Thank you. It's good to be back."

Marissa nodded. "I can imagine."

She returned to the counter, feeling a subtle satisfaction settle in her chest. She had crossed an invisible line: she wasn't just being welcomed anymore—she was helping welcome others.

When the morning rush thinned, Marissa untied her apron and hung it carefully on its hook. Caleb was already waiting by the door.

They stepped outside together. The sky had brightened, the harbor vivid and shining. The air carried salt and something sweet drifting from the bakery vents.

They walked unhurriedly.

"Do you ever stop and realize how different things feel?" Marissa asked.

"All the time," Caleb said. "But especially when you're near."

She smiled. "That wasn't subtle."

"I'm done trying to be."

They reached the end of the dock, the water stretching as far as the eye could see. The town was fully awake, but a sense of serenity still prevailed. They stood close, not touching yet connected. The water rippled softly below them, sunlight scattering into gentle gold.

"Does it scare you?" she asked. "Letting yourself care again?"

"Yes," he said without a beat. "But not enough to stop."

She exhaled slowly. "I'm not in a hurry," she said. "For labels. For promises."

"Neither am I."

Marissa's story didn't change with a single dramatic moment. It had shifted quietly.

Through presence. Through courage. Through the steady act of remaining.

And in the gentle glow of Mahone Bay, she understood that her new beginning wasn't imminent anymore.

She was living it.

• • • •

THAT EVENING, MARISSA returned to her rental as the sun dipped low over the harbor, splashing shades of rose and gold across the sky. She unlocked the door and stepped inside, noticing—really noticing—how different the space now looked.

Sophie's flowers sat on the small dining table in a blue glass vase she'd bought at the market. The canvas tote bag with the lighthouse hung on a hook by the door. Her sketchbook lay open on the coffee table, a half-finished drawing of the harbor visible. A coffee mug—one she'd claimed as her own from the rental's mismatched collection—sat washed and waiting by the sink.

Small changes. But they added up to something that felt unmistakably like *hers*.

She made tea and carried it to the window, watching the harbor lights blink on one by one across the bay. The same view she watched on her first night there, when the quiet had felt like absence, and the future had felt like a question she wasn't ready to answer.

Now, the quiet felt like peace.

She opened her journal—the pages no longer mostly empty—and wrote:

Six weeks ago, I arrived not knowing if I could stay. Today I can't imagine leaving. I think this is what home feels like.

She set down the pen and looked out at the water once more. The lacklusterness she'd seen in her rearview mirror that first day—the exhaustion of trying to prove her worth, of making herself small, of constantly running herself into the ground—was gone.

In its place was something she'd almost forgotten how to recognize.

Contentment.

Not because everything was perfect. Not because all her questions were answered. But because she stopped running and started choosing.

And Mahone Bay had chosen her back.

She closed the journal and smiled at her reflection in the darkened window—not a stranger anymore but someone she was beginning to recognize.

• • • •

Did you enjoy your visit to Mahone Bay? Harborlight Seasons is a heartwarming coastal romance series set in the charming seaside community of Mahone Bay, nestled along the windswept shores of Nova Scotia. Spanning seasons and stories, the series brings together tender journeys of hope, belonging, and unexpected love. Each book invites readers into a world shaped by community, kindness, and the quiet magic of fresh beginnings. As the tides shift and the seasons change, the residents of Mahone Bay face their own crossroads: returning home after heartbreak, rediscovering courage after loss, opening their hearts to new family, or realizing that the love they've been searching for has been waiting just around the corner. With memorable characters, emotional warmth, and a vivid sense of place, Harborlight Seasons offers an intimate glimpse into a town where every sunrise brings a new chance to heal, hope, and start again.

• • • •

Coming Home to Mahone Bay (Harborlights Seasons Book 1)
After losing her job and her confidence, Maren Sullivan returns to Mahone Bay—the town she left years ago—to help her aunt run the family café. However, the bay still holds memories of the man she never quite forgot. Jake Bennett has built his life by the water, repairing boats and keeping his heart safely anchored after being left behind once before. Seeing Maren again stirs feelings he thought he had buried deep. He isn't willing to risk reopening old wounds, especially when Maren is already planning her next escape. Will she realize that the home she's been looking for has been right here all along?

• • • •

A New Beginning at Mahone Bay (Harborlights Seasons Book 2)
Stories of Mahone Bay (Harborlights Seasons Book 3)
Café by Mahone Bay (Harborlights Seasons Book 4)
A Mahone Bay Christmas (Harborlights Seasons Book 5)

THANK YOU, READERS!

Thank you for reading this book. It is important to me to share my stories with you and that you enjoy them. May I ask a favor of you? If you enjoyed this book, would you please take a moment to leave a review? Thank you for your support!

Also, each week, I send my readers updates about my life as well as information about my new releases, freebies, promos, and book recommendations. If you're interested in receiving my weekly newsletter, please go to newsletter.sylviaprice.com[1], and it will ask you for your email. As a thank-you, you will receive several FREE exclusive short stories that aren't available for purchase!

Blessings,

Sylvia

---

1. http://newsletter.sylviaprice.com

Other Books by Sylvia Price

Finding Healing (Rainbow Haven Beach Prequel)

Available for FREE

Discover the power of second chances in this heartwarming series about love, loss, and a fresh start from bestselling author Sylvia Price.

Beth Campbell is a widow battling depression after losing her husband to cancer. As she stands over her husband's grave, she wishes that things had turned out differently. But when her childhood friend, Kathy, invites her to visit their hometown in Nova Scotia and help renovate an old house, she finds herself embarking on a journey that will change her life forever.

When Beth discovers that Sean Pennington, a man from her past, is working on the same project, she is determined to avoid him. As she begins to forget about the pain of losing her husband, Beth starts to realize that God may have bigger plans for her than just going back to the city and living her life in misery.

Join Beth on her journey of self-discovery and forgiveness. This inspirational series will touch your heart and remind you that it's never too late to start again. It is perfect for fans of uplifting women's fiction and readers who enjoy stories of finding hope and joy in unexpected places.

Songbird Cottage Beginnings (Pleasant Bay Prequel)

Available for FREE

Set on Canada's picturesque Cape Breton Island, this book is perfect for those who enjoy new beginnings and countryside landscapes.

Sam MacAuley and his wife Annalize are total opposites. When Sam wants to leave city life in Halifax to get a plot of land on Cape Breton Island, where he grew up, his wife wants nothing to do with his plans and opts to move herself and their three boys back to her home country of South Africa.

As Sam settles into a new life on his own, his friend Lachlan encourages him to get back into the dating scene. Although he meets plenty of women, he longs to find the one with whom he wants to share the rest of his life. Will Sam ever meet "the one"?

Get to know Sam and discover the origins of the Songbird Cottage.

This is the prequel to the rest of the Pleasant Bay series.

The Crystal Crescent Inn Boxed Set (Sambro Lighthouse Complete Series Collection)

Sylvia Price's Sambro Lighthouse Series, set on Canada's picturesque Crystal Crescent Beach, is a feel-good read perfect for fans of second chances with a bit of history and mystery all rolled into one. Enjoy all five sweet romance books in one collection for the first time!

Liz Beckett is grief-stricken when her beloved husband of thirty-five years dies after a long battle with cancer. Her daughter and best friend insist she needs a project to keep her occupied. Liz decides to share the beauty of Crystal Crescent Beach with those who visit the beautiful east coast of Nova Scotia and prepares to embark on the adventure of her life. She moves into the converted art studio at the bottom of her garden and turns the old family home into The Crystal Crescent Inn. One of her first visitors is famous archeologist, Merc MacGill, and he's not there to admire the view. The handsome bachelor believes there's an undiscovered eighteenth-century farmstead hidden inside the creeks and coves of Crystal Crescent, and Liz wants to help him find it.

But it's not all smooth sailing at the inn that overlooks the historic Sambro Lighthouse. No one has realized it yet, but the lives of everyone in Liz's family are intertwined with those first settlers who landed in Nova Scotia over two hundred and fifty years ago. Will they be able to unravel the mystery? Will the lives of Liz's two children be changed forever if they discover the link between the lighthouse and their old home?

Take a trip to Crystal Crescent Beach and join Liz, her family, and guests as they navigate the storms and calm waters of life and love under the watchful eye of the lighthouse and its secret.

A Seed of Hope (Hearts of Harmony Hill Prequel)

Available for FREE

In the tranquil Amish community of Harmony Hill, nestled in the rolling hills of Lancaster County, Sarah Stoltzfus and Ezekiel King begin their life together, bound by love and faith. Set a generation before the events of the main series, A Seed of Hope follows the heartwarming journey of Sarah and Ezekiel as they face the challenges of farming life, raising a family, and reconciling their individual dreams with the commitments they've made to each other and their community. As they navigate economic hardships and conflicting visions for their future, Sarah and Ezekiel's faith and devotion are tested. Will Sarah and Ezekiel's love be strong enough to overcome the trials ahead and plant the seeds of hope for future generations?

A Seed of Hope is a tender story of enduring love, faith, and the beginnings of a family legacy. In this prequel to the Hearts of Harmony Hill series, readers will be reminded how even the smallest seeds of hope can grow into something lasting.

Unexpected Gifts (Amish Hearts in Hopewell Prequel)

Available for FREE

In the heart of Hopewell, Indiana, Gabriel Miller tends to his farm, embracing the solitary life he's carved out for himself. But three unexpected visitors, accompanied by a stranger bearing news of his cousin's untimely passing, disrupt his quiet existence. With no one else to turn to, Gabriel takes on the responsibility of raising the orphaned children. Alone and overwhelmed, he grapples with the daunting task of managing his farm while becoming a caregiver to three young souls. In this tale of unexpected responsibilities and unspoken desires, Anna Burkholder emerges as a beacon of hope. Stepping in to care for the children during the day, Anna, who harbors an unspoken affection for Gabriel, finds herself entangled in a situation that might just offer her a chance at capturing his attention. As Anna and Gabriel navigate the complexities of raising a family, they discover that love has a way of blossoming in the most unforeseen places.

Will their newfound roles bring them closer together, or will the weight of their responsibilities tear them apart? Join Gabriel and Anna on a journey of resilience, sacrifice, and the transformative power of love as they navigate the challenges of building an unconventional family.

Unexpected Gifts is the prequel to the *Amish Hearts in Hopewell* series, and in it, you will be introduced to the characters who appear throughout the series.

The Bridge of Dreams (Lancaster Bridges Prequel)

Available for FREE

Discover a world of love, faith, and community in this prequel to an exciting Amish romance series. Follow the Lancaster County Amish as they navigate the challenges of balancing their beliefs with the allure of the wider world.

In a world where expectations and traditions are highly valued, eldest daughter Hannah Fisher's dream of attending college creates a rift within her Amish community. As Hannah struggles to find a balance between her Amish faith and her desire to explore the outside world, tensions rise, and relationships are put to the test. To complicate matters further, Samuel Stoltzfus, Hannah's childhood friend, has his heart set on courting her, making it even harder for her to choose her path.

Meanwhile, younger sister Ruth struggles to reconcile her own dreams with the expectations of the community. Follow Hannah and her sister Ruth through their journey of self-discovery as they navigate the conflict between tradition and change with unexpected twists and turns along the way.

The Lancaster Bridges series explores a close-knit Amish community in Pennsylvania as they navigate the challenges of a rapidly changing world.

Experience the beauty and simplicity of Amish culture, while also witnessing the characters' journeys of self-discovery, personal growth, and community building. Overall, the series offers a rich and heartfelt portrayal of a community that is both deeply traditional and open to change, and celebrates the enduring values of family, faith, and love.

Sarah (The Amish of Morrissey County Prequel)

Available for FREE

Welcome to Morrissey County! This fictional region in Pennsylvania Amish country is home to several generations of strong-willed Amish women who know what they want in life, even if others disagree. Join these women on their search for love and acceptance.

Morrissey County, 1979

Sarah Kauffman has always abided by the *Ordnung*, and not only because her father happens to be the town's bishop and would, she feels, disown her if she didn't. But when her mother passes away, she longs to escape the clutches of her father and run away to the *Englisch* world. When her father wants her to marry someone she doesn't love, Sarah becomes even more desperate to leave.

Jacob Renno, on the other hand, is happy with life on his farm. It keeps him so busy that the older bachelor has no time for love, but on lonely nights, he finds himself longing for a companion.

When Sarah and Jacob meet, there's an instant connection, but things get complicated. Jacob offers to help Sarah with her dilemma, but Bishop Kaufmann insists that she obey his wishes. Will Sarah run off to join the *Englisch*, or will the handsome farmer give her pause? Will her father disown her or give her his blessing? Find out in this sweet Amish romance as you become immersed in the lives of these Morrissey County residents.

Sarah is the prequel to the Amish of Morrissey County series. Each book is a stand-alone read, but to make the most of the series, you should consider reading them in order.

The Origins of Cardinal Hill (The Amish of Cardinal Hill Prequel)

Available for FREE

Two girls with a legacy to carry on. A third choosing to forge her own path.

Welcome to Cardinal Hill, Indiana! This quaint fictional town is home to Faith Hochstetler, Leah Bontrager, Iris Mast, their families, and their trades. Faith, Leah, and Iris are united in their shared passion for turning their hobbies within nature into profitable businesses...and finding love! Find out how it all begins in this short, free prequel!

Other books in this series:

- *The Beekeeper's Calendar*: Faith's Story
- *The Soapmaker's Recipe*: Leah's Story
- *The Herbalist's Remedy*: Iris's Story

The Origins of Cardinal Hill is the prequel to the Amish of Cardinal Hill series. Each book is a stand-alone read, but to make the most of the series, you should consider reading them in order.

A Promised Tomorrow (The Yoder Family Saga Prequel)

Available for FREE

The Yoder Family Saga follows widow Miriam Yoder and her four unmarried daughters, Megan, Rebecca, Josephine, and Lillian, as they discover God's plans for them and the hope He provides for a happy tomorrow.

The Yoder women struggle to survive after Jeremiah Yoder succumbs to a battle with cancer. The family risks losing their farm and their livelihood. They are desperate to find a way to keep going. Will Miriam and her daughters be able to work together to keep their family afloat? Will God pull through for them and provide for them in their time of need?

A Promised Tomorrow is the prequel to the Yoder Family Saga. Join the Yoder women through their journey of loss and hope for a better future. Each book is a stand-alone read, but to make the most of the series, you should consider reading them in order. Start reading this sweet Amish romance today that will take you on a rollercoaster of emotions as you're welcomed into the life of the Yoder family.

Jonah's Redemption: Book 1

Available for FREE

Jonah has lost his community, and he's struggling to get by in the English world. He yearns for his Amish roots, but his past mistakes keep him from returning home.

Mary Lou is recovering from a medical scare. Her journey has impressed upon her how precious life is, so she decides to go on *rumspringa* to see the world.

While in the city, Mary Lou meets Jonah. Unable to understand his foul attitude, especially towards her, she makes every effort to share her faith with him. As she helps him heal from his past, an attraction develops.

Will Jonah's heart soften towards Mary Lou? What will God do with these two broken people?

The Christmas Cards: An Amish Holiday Romance

Lucy Yoder is a young Amish widow who recently lost the love of her life, Albrecht. As Christmas approaches, she dreads what was once her favorite holiday, knowing that this Christmas was supposed to be the first one she and Albrecht shared together. Then, one December morning, Lucy discovers a Christmas card from an anonymous sender on her doorstep. Lucy receives more cards, all personal, all tender, all comforting. Who in the shadows is thinking of her at Christmas?

Andy Peachey was born with a rare genetic disorder. Coming to grips with his predicament makes him feel a profound connection to Lucy Yoder. Seeking meaning in life, he uses his talents to give Christmas cheer. Will Andy's efforts touch Lucy's heart and allow her to smile again? Or will Lucy, herself, get in his way?

The Christmas Cards is a story of loss and love and the ability to find yourself again in someone else.

About the Author

SYLVIA PRICE IS AN author of Amish and contemporary romance and women's fiction. She especially loves writing uplifting stories about second chances!

Sylvia was inspired to write about the Amish as a result of the enduring legacy of Mennonite missionaries in her life. While living with them for three weeks, they got her a library card and encouraged her to start reading to cope with the loss of television and radio, Sylvia developed a newfound appreciation for books.

Although raised in the cosmopolitan city of Montréal, Sylvia spent her adolescent and young adult years in Nova Scotia, and the beautiful countryside landscapes and ocean views serve as the backdrop to her contemporary novels.

After meeting and falling in love with an American while living abroad, Sylvia now resides in the US. She spends her days writing, hoping to inspire the next generation to read more stories. When she's not writing, Sylvia stays busy making sure her three young children are alive and well-fed.

• • • •

FOLLOW SYLVIA ON FACEBOOK at http://facebook.com/sylviapriceauthor for updates.

Join Sylvia's Advanced Reader Copies (ARC) team at http://arcteam.sylviaprice.com[1] to get her books for free before they are released in exchange for honest reviews.

• • • •

SUBSCRIBE TO SYLVIA'S newsletter at http://newsletter.sylviaprice.com[2] to get to know Sylvia and her family. It's also a great way to stay in the loop about new releases, freebies, promos, and more.

As a thank-you, you will receive several FREE exclusive short stories that are not available for purchase.

1. http://arcteam.sylviaprice.com/

2. http://newsletter.sylviaprice.com/

HOPE
for Hannah's
LOVE
Amish Love Through the Seasons
SHORT STORY
SYLVIA PRICE

SYLVIA PRICE
EVE
AN ELIJAH COMPANION STORY

www.ingramcontent.com/pod-product-compliance
Lightning Source LLC
Chambersburg PA
CBHW022117010526
44274CB00010B/470
* 9 7 9 8 2 3 3 8 4 5 3 3 8 *